Dreams of a Rocking Pony

ILLUSTRATED BY

Peggy Mory

WRITTEN BY

Terah Van Dusen

LUMINARE PRESS
WWW.LUMINAREPRESS.COM

Illustrations by Peggy Mory
Cover design by Claire Flint Last

Luminare Press
442 Charnelton St.
Eugene, OR 97401
www.luminarepress.com

LCCN: 2020925286
ISBN: 978-1-64388-601-5

To autumn
NELL

Love
GRANNY Peg

I dreamed I met a cowgirl squirrel,
my what a rope she could twirl!

I dreamed of a great horned owl,
sun high in the sky,
we rode through town.

I dreamed of a trick skunk,
black and white,
together at last,
we wore our stripes.

I dreamed of a desert-loving lizard,
they said their favorite food was gizzards.

I dreamed a raccoon jumped on top,
moving too fast,
a cop made us stop.

I dreamed of a dancing cat
with a fist full of feathers,
she was standing on my saddle
made of leather.

I dreamed a mouse
grabbed on to my tail,
through the starry
night we sailed.

I dreamed a rabbit
turned me brown,
together we galloped
underground.

I dreamed that inside my stirrup
a bird built a nest,
making a home for
her eggs to hatch.

I dreamed I was overcome with pride,
when I gave a baby javelina his first ride.

I dreamed a jockey fox was on my back,
we raced together around the track.

I dreamed a horned lizard took a spin,
my horse tail whooshing in the wind.

Peggy Mory is a professional painter who works with acrylic and multimedia. This is her first time illustrating a book. She was born in Fort Worth, Texas, and resides near Tucson, Arizona.

Terah Van Dusen writes and lives on a farm in the Willamette Valley near Eugene, Oregon. Her blog, *Mama Bird*, can be found at www.terahvandusen.com.

Peggy Mory is Terah Van Dusen's grandmother. They created this book together shortly after Terah's daughter, Autumn, was born.

Made in the USA
Las Vegas, NV
11 September 2021